For Austin
– C.D.

For Eli
– N.Z.J.

First published in 2009 by Scholastic Inc
This edition first published in 2010 by Scholastic Children's Books
Euston House, 24 Eversholt Street
London NW1 1DB
a division of Scholastic Ltd
www.scholastic.co.uk

London ~ New York ~ Toronto ~ Sydney ~ Auckland
Mexico City ~ New Delhi ~ Hong Kong

Text copyright © 2009 Corinne Demas
Illustrations copyright © 2009 Noah Z. Jones

ISBN 978 1407 11499 6

ALWAYS IN TROUBLE

Written by Corinne Demas & Illustrated by Noah Z. Jones

SCHOLASTIC

Emma's dog, Toby, was always in trouble.

On Monday, he got into the rubbish.

On Tuesday, he ran into the road.

On Wednesday, he ate a loaf of bread that Emma's dad had just baked.

On Thursday, he barked in the middle of the night.

On Friday, he wet the rug.

On Saturday, he chewed up all the buttons on Emma's new coat.

On Sunday, he snoozed.

But on Monday morning he got into the rubbish again.

"Something has to be done about that dog!"
said Emma's mum.

"Maybe he isn't getting
enough attention," said Emma.

So all day on Monday she gave Toby lots of attention.

She took him for walks...

and brushed his fur...

... and sang him silly songs.

But on Tuesday Toby ate a box of crayons.

On Wednesday, he jumped into the basket of clean laundry that Emma's mum had just finished folding.

He was very good on Thursday.

He was very good on Friday.

But on Saturday he chewed up a magazine.

And on Sunday he rolled around in some mud and then ran across the clean kitchen floor.

"Something has to be done about that dog!"
cried Emma's mum.

"Maybe he needs to go to dog training school," said Emma.

"What a great idea!" said Emma's mum.

The first class started the next day.

There were ten dogs in Toby's class.

Some were big and some were little. Some barked
and some yipped and some growled and some whined.

Toby was quiet as a goldfish.

He behaved perfectly at school every week,
and he did everything just right.

When Emma said "Sit!"
he sat.

When Emma said "Come!"
he came.

When Emma said "Heel!"
he stood right by her side.

"He was the best dog," said Ms. Katz, the teacher, when the classes were all over. At graduation she gave Toby a certificate with a gold seal.

Emma's mum taped the certificate low down on the wall, right over Toby's dog dish. "Now you know how to behave," she said to Toby.

But on Monday, Toby got into the rubbish.

On Tuesday, he ran into the road.

On Wednesday, he ate the biscuits that Emma's dad had just baked.

On Thursday, he barked in the middle of the night and woke everyone up.

On Friday, he wet the rug.

On Saturday, he dug up the petunias Emma and her mum had just planted.

On Sunday, he chewed up his certificate.

"Something has to be done about that dog!"
cried Emma's mum.

Emma took him back to dog school.

"Does he sit?"
asked Ms. Katz.

"Yes," said Emma.

"Does he come?"
asked Ms. Katz.

"Yes," said Emma.

"Does he heel?"
asked Ms. Katz.

"Yes," said Emma.

"Well then, what's
the trouble?"
asked Ms. Katz.

So Emma told her.

"I see," said Ms. Katz. "If you want a specially trained dog, you'll have to leave him with me for the week."

"OK," said Emma.

Emma missed Toby all week. He was very happy to see her when she picked him up.

"I hope you've learned something this time,"
said Emma's mum.

"Please, Toby," Emma whispered to him,
"you've got to be good now."

Toby licked Emma's face. He had a strange
twinkle in his eye.

On Monday, he took out the rubbish.

On Tuesday, he baked some bread.

On Wednesday, he vacuumed the rug.

On Thursday, he folded the laundry.

On Friday, he washed the kitchen floor.

On Saturday, he planted some petunias.

And on Sunday he snoozed.

But no dog can be perfect always – not even Toby.